# The Dove's Letter

## Written and illustrated by

# KEITH BAKER

Harcourt Brace & Company

San Diego    New York    London

Printed in Hong Kong

Requests for permission to make copies of any
part of the work should be mailed to
Permissions Department,
Harcourt Brace & Company, 8th Floor,
Orlando, Florida 32887.

Library of Congress Cataloging-in-Publication Data
Baker, Keith, 1953–
The dove's letter.
Summary: As a dove tries to deliver an unaddressed
letter to its rightful owner, she brings
great pleasure to each person who reads it.
[1. Letters — Fiction.    2. Pigeons — Fiction.]
I. Title.
PZ7.B17427Do    1988      [E]      87-8530
ISBN 0-15-224133-7
ISBN 0-15-224134-5 (pbk.)

A B C D E
B C D E F (pbk.)

The illustrations in this book were done in Liquitex acrylics on illustration board.
The text type was set in Raleigh Medium by Thompson Type, San Diego, California.
The display type was hand-lettered by Judythe Sieck.
Printed and bound by South China Printing Co., Ltd., Hong Kong
Production supervision by Warren Wallerstein and Ginger Boyer
Designed by Judythe Sieck

*For my parents*

A perfect day for flying," thought the dove.

The air was so clear and the sun so bright that the dove could count the petals on the wildflowers below. But something caught her eye that was not a wildflower. It lay square and silent upon the ground.

"Whose letter is this?" wondered the dove. There was no name on the envelope—not even a stamp—so the dove untied the ribbon from around the letter. A page with elegant writing on delicate paper unfolded before her.

"This letter must be special. I will give it a special delivery."

And the dove flew away to see who she might see.

*Whoosh-chop! Whoosh-chop!* The dove heard a woodsman working below. She flew down to meet him.

"A letter for me?" the woodsman asked. He opened it gently. Then he smiled a smile as wide as the wedge he had cut in the trunk of the tree.

"My wife wrote this letter. She wears a ribbon of the same color, and this morning she tied it in her hair."

Then the woodsman ran off. He was so excited that he forgot not only his ax, but the letter as well.

"Maybe it's his, and maybe it isn't," thought the dove. "Something this special should not be left behind." Away she flew to see who she might see.

"Carrots, pumpkins, and peas—I've grown every vegetable you please!" sang the farmer. The dove flew down to meet her.

"My scarecrow doesn't seem to be working," laughed the farmer. "And who is this from?" she asked, taking the letter. "It's covered with chips of wood and it smells like the forest."

As the farmer read, an expression as bright and full as a sunflower blossomed across her face.

"My brother wrote this. He is a carpenter and builds with wood from the forest nearby. I'm sure this came from his shop."

She pressed the letter over her heart. "I'd hug him, too, if he were here." As the farmer picked up her basket and rushed away, the letter fell from her pocket.

"Was it hers?" the dove wondered. "Something this special should not be left behind." And away she flew to see who she might see.

Sweet and savory aromas drew the dove to a baker delivering a batch of steaming pies.

"The mail is early today," said the baker. He took the letter with his flour-covered hands. "Oh, look—there's a button shape pressed into the paper."

As he read, a tear of joy as big as a blueberry rolled down his cheek.

"My daughter made this letter. Her dress has a button just like the one used here. Now I'll surprise her!" The baker grabbed the biggest pie and ran off—without the letter.

"Was it his? Something this special should not be left behind," thought the dove, and away she flew to see who she might see.

*Clip, a-clop, clip, a-clop.* A white horse was a lucky sign, so the dove flew down to meet the rider.

"Are you the new mail carrier?" the rider asked when the dove gave her the letter. She quickly began to read, and her eyes lit up like the noonday sun.

"There's flour all over this—my mother must have written it.

Today is her baking day; she should be taking loaves of hot bread out of the oven just now."

The rider turned her horse and galloped away. The dove was thrown high into the air, and the letter fell to the muddy road.

"Oh, I still have the letter," thought the dove, "and something this special should not be left behind." Away she flew to see who she might see.

"Over, under, back, and through, I weave to make a gift for you," chanted the weaver. The dove landed on her window box.

"Since when does my mail come from the sky?" asked the weaver. "And why is this letter covered with dirt?"

When she read, her cheeks grew as red as two balls of crimson yarn.

"Of course, my son made this. He loves to play in the mud, and he's always making things. I'll give him the scarf I've just woven."

*Snip, clip, snap.* The weaver cut the scarf from the loom and hurried away. The letter lay among the trimmings of her weaving.

The search had grown long, but the dove knew she must continue. So away she flew to see who she might see.

The dove heard the humming of a potter's wheel. The potter raised his head as she flew toward him.

"That fluttering sounds like a dove," said the blind potter. The dove put the letter in his open hands. The potter touched and felt it tenderly. "Say, there's a piece of yarn in this letter." Then he smiled a smile as big as one of his clay pots.

"My friend is sending me a message. She is knitting a sweater for me from this same wool." The potter ran off without finishing the bowl and without taking the letter.

All day long the letter had been left behind. Soon the sun would set. The dove began her flight home.

"A traveler—no, a soldier—is walking below.

But it is too late, and I am too sleepy to stop."

"But maybe the letter is his." As the dove flew toward the soldier, she startled him.

"Get away! Don't bother me! I am tired, and I have many more miles to go before dark. Why should I get a letter? People have forgotten me." But the soldier took the letter and read slowly.

"No, this is not mine. I have been in battle for many years. I had forgotten about the feelings written here, though once I knew them well. This letter reminds me of so many people. It gives me hope. Please, let me take it to someone I once loved."

But the dove did not hear. She had fallen asleep.

"You must have been searching a long time," the soldier said.

"I shall take you home."

The dove slept late into the next morning. When she awoke, she found many gifts, but where did they come from?

Then she remembered the woodsman, the farmer, the baker, the horse and rider, the weaver, and the potter. But she could not find the letter.

"Oh yes," thought the dove, "the soldier." She had delivered the letter after all.

At the same time and not too far away, the soldier thought only of the

dove and the letter and the special delivery he was about to make.